A CENTURY
OF STORIES
NEW HANOVER COUNTY PUBLIC LIBRARY
1906-2006

MOTORCYCLE RACING
The Fast Track

Supermoto

JIM MEZZANOTTE

Please visit our web site at: www.garethstevens.com
For a free color catalog describing Gareth Stevens Publishing's
list of high-quality books and multimedia programs, call
1-800-542-2595 (USA) or 1-800-387-3178 (Canada).
Gareth Stevens Publishing's fax: (414) 332-3567.

Library of Congress Cataloging-in-Publication Data

Mezzanotte, Jim.
    Supermoto / by Jim Mezzanotte.
      p. cm. — (Motorcycle racing: The fast track)
    Includes bibliographical references and index.
    ISBN 0-8368-6426-3 (lib. bdg.)
    ISBN 0-8368-6575-8 (softcover)
    1. Supercross—Juvenile literature. I. Title.
  GV1060.1455.M49   2006
  796.7'56—dc22   2005027218

This edition first published in 2006 by
Gareth Stevens Publishing
A Member of the WRC Media Family of Companies
330 West Olive Street, Suite 100
Milwaukee, WI 53212 USA

Editor: Leifa Butrick
Cover design and layout: Dave Kowalski
Art direction: Tammy West
Picture research: Diane Laska-Swanke

Technical Advisor: Kerry Graeber

Photo credits: Cover, pp. 9, 11, 13, 17 © Mike Doran/D&W Images; pp. 5, 7, 15,
19, 21 © Brian J. Nelson

Printed in the United States of America

1 2 3 4 5 6 7 8 9 10 09 08 07 06

CONTENTS

Cover: A rider catches air during a supermoto race.
Supermoto has all kinds of racing action.

The World of Supermoto

Who is the best motorcycle racer? The question is tough to answer. There are many kinds of motorcyle racing. They are all different.

In the 1970s, a new kind of U.S. racing began. It tried to answer the question — who is the best? It was called the Superbiker series. It combined different kinds of racing. Some racers came from **motocross**. Others came from **flat track racing** or **road racing**.

After awhile, this type of racing ended. Then it caught on in Europe. There, it was called *supermotard*, which is French for "superbiker." Today, it is back in the United States. It is now called supermoto. This popular sport is many kinds of racing in one!

Supermoto combines different kinds of racing.
One kind is road racing, with twisting turns.

Pavement
and Dirt

A supermoto race is held on a special track. The track has paved parts and dirt parts. It has different parts for different kinds of racing.

The dirt part has jumps, like a motocross track. The paved part has straightaways and twisting turns, like a road racing track. It also has wide, sweeping turns, like a flat track.

Supermoto races can be held in all kinds of places. Some are held in parking lots. Others are held on tracks used for car racing. Sometimes, a track is laid out in a city. The riders race through the streets!

A rider flies over a dirt jump. In a short time, the rider will be on a paved section.

Supermoto Races

The AMA Supermoto Championship is a U.S. racing series. AMA Pro Racing sets the rules for the races. It is part of the American Motorcyclist Association, or AMA. These races are for **pros**, but there are many supermoto races for **amateurs**, too.

Pro riders earn points for how they finish in each race. The last race is the championship finale. After this race, all the points are added. The rider with the most points is the champ.

In a supermoto event, riders first **qualify** to compete. They get timed as they race around the track. They also compete in qualifying races, called heats. The fastest riders go on to the final race, called the main event.

On a city street, riders begin a supermoto race. Only the fastest riders get to compete.

Special Bikes

A supermoto bike has a tough job. It must handle high speeds on pavement. It must also handle jumps and turns on dirt. Some companies make bikes just for supermoto racing. Most people **modify** motocross bikes for supermoto.

Motocross bikes have knobby tires. The big knobs dig into the dirt, but the tires are not good on pavement. Supermoto bikes use tires with no knobs. These **slicks** work well on both dirt and pavement. Riders sometimes cut grooves in the tires. With grooves, the tires grip the ground better. The bikes also have bigger, more powerful brakes.

Riders modify their engines, too. A modified engine produces a lot more **horsepower**.

This bike is just for supermoto racing. It uses slicks instead of knobby tires.

Safety Gear

In supermoto races, riders sometimes crash. Dirt gets onto the pavement, making it slippery. The riders jump high in the air. They travel very fast on straightaways. They may bump into each other and fall. Riders need a lot of protection.

Riders wear helmets to protect their heads. They wear goggles to protect their eyes. They wear pads for their elbows and knees, and gloves for their hands. Some riders wear leather clothing. These "leathers" protect them if they hit pavement. Others wear clothing used in motocross. Riders also wear boots with metal toes to protect their feet.

A rider slides through a turn. Riders have a lot of protection in case they fall.

Many Skills

Most riders learn skills for one kind of racing. In supermoto, they learn many kinds of skills.

Riders have to jump. They have to travel over big humps, called rollers. Riders must stay upright and balanced on the loose dirt. In some turns, they put a foot to the ground and let the rear wheel slide around.

Racing on pavement can be tricky. Coming off a dirt section, the tires may be full of dirt. It gets on the pavement. This dirt is slippery, so riders must be careful. Their bikes reach high speeds on pavement. In twisting turns, they lean to one side and then the other. They take the fastest line, or path, through turns.

In supermoto, riders need many skills. These riders must jump and then take a sharp turn.

A New Sport

Supermoto is very new in the United States, but the sport is getting bigger. The X Games have supermoto racing. Top pro riders race in U.S. supermoto.

Many pros come from other kinds of racing. In 2004, Jeff Ward was supermoto champ. He has been a star in motocross. Jeremy McGrath has raced in supermoto, too. He is a big **supercross** star. Other pros have won in flat track racing and road racing.

The sport keeps changing. Riders are still figuring out the best way to win. The bikes keep improving. Riders are learning new **techniques** to go faster.

Jeff Ward has won many motorcycle races. He has also raced cars.

Amateur Supermoto

U.S. amateur supermoto is getting popular, too. It has been around longer than pro racing. Riders of all ages compete. Whole families join the fun. Most riders use modified motocross bikes, like the pros. Local races are held in many areas.

The sport will probably keep growing. More people will enjoy watching the pros race. Some will want to race, too! More tracks will hold amateur races.

Many young riders love supermoto. Some also compete in motocross or other kinds of racing. Others only compete in supermoto. If they keep racing, they will only get better. A few may become pros. They will be tomorrow's stars!

Young riders compete in amateur supermoto. They may be racing for many years to come!

Let's Race!

Ready to race? You take your place on the **grid**. There are many rows of bikes and riders. An official waves a green flag. You're off! Many engines roar as you head for the first turn. You try to reach it before other riders.

First, you're on pavement. You slide around a corner. Then, you're on dirt. You hit a jump and fly through the air. After landing, you are back on pavement. Watch out for the loose dirt!

You speed down a straight and brake hard for a turn. An official waves a yellow flag. One of the riders has fallen — no passing. You keep going. Will you catch the leaders?

In supermoto, riders are often close together. It is a tight race to the finish.

GLOSSARY

amateurs: in sports, people who compete for fun and not to earn money.

flat track racing: a kind of motorcycle racing that takes place on flat oval tracks with dirt surfaces.

grid: the starting lineup on a racetrack. A grid usually has many rows of riders, with several riders in each row. Riders' places on the grid depend on how well they qualify.

horsepower: the amount of power an engine produces, based on how much work one horse can do.

modify: make changes to something.

motocross: a kind of motorcycle racing that takes place on outdoor tracks with hills, jumps, and other obstacles.

pros: in sports, people who earn money competing.

slicks: tires with a smooth tread, or surface. Road racing bikes and supermoto bikes use slicks.

qualify: in racing, to earn a spot in the main race.

road racing: a kind of motorcycle racing in which riders compete on paved tracks with twisting turns and high-speed straightaways.

supercross: a kind of motorcycle racing that is similar to motocross. It takes place inside sports stadiums, on dirt tracks with jumps and other obstacles.

techniques: methods or ways of doing things.

FURTHER INFORMATION

Books

Dirt Bikes. Motorcycle Mania (series). David Armentrout (Rourke Publishing)

Motocross. Radical Sports (series). Gary Freeman (Heinemann)

Dirt Track Racing. Motorcycles (series). Ed Youngblood (Capstone Press)

Motorcycle Grand Prix Racing. Action Sports (series). Joe Herran (Chelsea House)

Videos

This is Supermoto (Kultur)

Web Sites

www.amasupermoto.com
This web site is the official site for AMA supermoto racing. It has information about races and also has photos.

www.redbullcopilot.com
At this web site, click on "Red Bull Supermoto." You will be riding with supercross star Jeremy McGrath! This amazing site has many interactive features.

www.redbullsupermoto.com
Visit this site to learn all about the Red Bull Supermoto A-Go-Go. The site has information about riders and many action photos.

www.supermotousa.net
At this site, click on "photos" to see some pictures of amateur racing.

INDEX

ML

5/06